For our dear sister, Beth
who's reading level c
as her age increas
Happy 21st birthday!! ☺

Love,
Melinda, John & Geoffrey

JAMES STEVENSON

The Worst
Person
in the World
at
Crab Beach

Greenwillow Books, New York

Black pen and watercorlor paints were used to prepare the full-color art. The typeface is Zapf International Medium.

First edition   10 9 8 7 6 5 4 3 2 1

Library of Congress Cataloging-in-Publication Data

Stevenson, James (date)
The worst person in the world at Crab Beach.
Summary: The worst person is having a terrible time on his vacation but he becomes even more miserable after he meets Miriam and her son.
[1. Vacations—Fiction.   2. Humorous stories]   I. Title.
PZ7.S84748Wr 1988   [E]   86-31931
ISBN 0-688-07298-4   ISBN 0-688-07299-2 (lib. bdg.)

One morning in June, the worst person in the
world went out to water his poison ivy and weed
his cactus. He looked up at the sky. "Oh, no," he
said, "not another nice day!"
He heard birds singing and children playing.
He put his hands over his ears. "It's going to be
like this all summer!" he said.

He went back into his messy house and sat down
in his uncomfortable chair. "I need a vacation,"
he said. "But where?"
He looked at a map. At last he found a place not
far away called Crab Beach.
"Sounds good," said the worst person.

He made a sign and put it in the window.
He packed his bag with things he didn't want.
Then he put the bag and his umbrella on the
back of his old bicycle, and set off.

He rode his bicycle as fast as he could, never
slowing down for anybody. At last he came to
Crab Beach.
A cold fog covered everything.
He could hardly see. Then it began to drizzle.
"I *like* it here," said the worst person.
When he saw a ramshackle old hotel, he stopped.

"Would you like a room, sir?" asked the hotel clerk.

"I don't know," said the worst. "How are the mosquitoes here?"

"Very large, sir," said the clerk.

"Jellyfish?" asked the worst.

"Lots," said the clerk.

"Is it often cold and foggy?" asked the worst.

"In the daytime it is," said the clerk.

"How's the food?" asked the worst.

"Don't ask," said the clerk.

"What about the other guests?" asked the worst.
"Are they friendly and cheerful?"
"Not in the least," said the clerk.
"Give me a room," said the worst. "I'm staying."

He selected a room in the cellar. It had a hard
bed and no view whatsoever.

The next morning, the worst set out for a stroll.
The fog was thicker than ever. "No flowers, no
birds, no children, no friendly people," said the
worst. "This place is a real find."
Suddenly, he bumped into something. His hat
fell off, and his umbrella went flying.

THUMP!

"Clumsy fool!" cried a woman's voice. It was shrill
and screechy. "Watch where you're going, stupid!"
"Why don't *you*?" said the worst. "And stop
yelling!"

"You call that yelling?" said the woman. "That's not
yelling. Cranston, show the man what yelling is."
"This is yelling," said a child's voice. "CLUMSY
FOOOOL!" he screamed.
The worst person's ears rang and rang.

"Where's my umbrella?" said the worst, when
    he could hear again.
"Who cares?" said the woman.
"Is this stupid thing your hat?" said the child.
    The worst took the hat. "Perhaps it is," he said.
    Then he marched off down the beach.

When the worst got back to the hotel, he saw
a woman and a child. The child was holding
his umbrella.

"Yours, mister?" he asked.

"Yes," said the worst. "So don't think you can
steal it, you little twerp."

"Steal it?" said the woman. "You couldn't *give* this away." She grabbed the umbrella and turned it inside out.

"Who are those rude people?" asked the worst.

"Her name is Miriam," said the desk clerk, "and her son is named Cranston."

That night, the worst was awakened by a dreadful sound over his head. He couldn't get back to sleep, so he went upstairs.
He followed the sound to a certain door. He knocked.

Cranston opened the door. "What do *you* want?"
he said.

"Who is it?" said Miriam.

"It's that awful old man, Mama," said Cranston.

"What's all this racket?" said the worst.

"We're practicing our accordions," said Miriam.

"And *you're* interrupting us," said Cranston.

"I despise accordions," said the worst.

"Tough beans for you, mister," said Cranston,
and Miriam slammed the door.

The following day, the worst walked to the far end
of the beach for a picnic. He carried his sour
pickle sandwich in a brown paper bag.
He sat down on what he thought was an old crate.
There was a terrible wheezing sound.

"Mama!" shrieked Cranston. "That terrible man
  sat on your accordion!"
"The old fool probably broke it!" said Miriam.
  She picked it up and tested it.
"Nonsense," said the worst. "It sounds just as
  awful as ever."
"We came all the way down here so we could
  practice without being pestered by you," said
  Miriam.

"I came all the way down here so I could have my lunch without hearing *you*," said the worst, marching away.

He didn't see the sand castle until he tripped over it.

"My castle!" shrieked Cranston.

"Look what you did!" He ran down the beach howling "Mama, Mama!"

Miriam grabbed the worst's lunch and threw
it into the ocean. "Lunch is over," she said.
"Why don't you shove off?"

"My pickle sandwich!" cried the worst, watching it
sink slowly under the waves.

"I'm leaving!" he said.

"Not fast enough," said Cranston.

"'Rudolph the Red-Nosed Reindeer,'" said Miriam
to Cranston. "Take it from the top! One, two, and
three . . ."

The worst went back to the hotel, holding his ears.

The next morning, the worst peeked out his door
to make sure Miriam and Cranston weren't
around. Then he crept upstairs.
They weren't in the lobby, or on the porch.
"Good," said the worst, and set off on his walk.
The beach was all clear, too. "This is my lucky
day," said the worst.

When he went to bed that night, he listened
carefully for annoying sounds. There weren't any.

There was heavy rain the next morning, so the worst decided to go into the village. He looked at a store window for a while. Then he went inside. When he came out he was wearing a new hat. He threw his old hat away and rode back to the hotel.

"Not that it matters," said the worst to the hotel
   clerk, "but what's become of that dreadful
   Miriam and her horrible little boy?"
"Oh, they checked out," said the clerk.
"Where did they go?" asked the worst.
"Beats me," said the clerk. "New hat?"
   That night the worst had trouble sleeping. He
   thrashed and squirmed, and in the morning
   he decided to leave.

"Come and see us again, hear?" said the clerk.

"Not in a million years," said the worst.

He packed, got on his bicycle, and started for home.

"What nerve that Miriam and Cranston have," he
said to himself. "Annoying me by making me
think they were still around to annoy me. . . .
Vacation is even worse than no vacation," he
thought as he went down the road.

Later in the day he was passing a hotel when he
heard music. He stopped his bicycle. It sounded
like accordion music.
He listened for a moment. It *was* accordion music.
He hurried up the steps and into the hotel.

A small orchestra was playing, and people
were having tea.
"May I help you, sir?" asked a waiter.
"No!" said the worst person, and left.

He bicycled home as fast as he could.
"Get out of my way!" he cried to anyone he saw.
When he got to his house he heard noises in
his yard.
"Who's in there?" he cried.

"Us," said Miriam.

"What are *you* doing here?" said the worst.

"Cranston's watering your poison ivy," said Miriam,
"and I'm weeding your cactus garden."

"Oh," said the worst. "Do you live around here?"

"A few blocks away," said Miriam.

"I walk past your house every day on the way to
  school," said Cranston.

"I never saw you," said the worst.

"That's because I saw you first," said Cranston.

"What's that on your head?" said Miriam.

"I bought a new hat," said the worst.

"It's almost as stupid as the old one," said Cranston.

"Oh," said the worst.

"But not quite," said Miriam.

"No, not quite," said Cranston.

"Would you care for a dry cracker and a glass of prune juice?" asked the worst. "Might not hurt," said Miriam. They sat on the porch and ate dry crackers and drank prune juice.

"Where are my <u>GO AWAY</u> and <u>KEEP OUT</u> signs?"
  asked the worst.
"We took them down," said Miriam.
"You won't need them when *we're* around,"
  said Cranston.
"You're probably right," said the worst.
"More prune juice?"